This book is to be returned on or before
the last date stamped below.

A MEDAL FOR POPPY

The Pluckiest Pig in the World

Rose Impey
Shoo Rayner

ORCHARD BOOKS

ORCHARD BOOKS
96 Leonard Street, London EC2A 4RH
Orchard Books Australia
14 Mars Road, Lane Cove, NSW 2066
First published in Great Britain in 1998
First paperback edition 1999
Text © Rose Impey 1998
Illustrations © Shoo Rayner 1998
The right of Rose Impey to be identified as the
Author and Shoo Rayner as the Illustrator of this Work
has been asserted by them in accordance with the
Copyright, Designs and Patents Act, 1988.
A CIP catalogue record for this book is
available from the British Library.
1 86039 619 4 (hardback)
1 86039 878 2 (paperback)
Printed in Great Britain.

A MEDAL FOR POPPY

Old Man Brocksopp had a farm,
Eee-Aye, Eee-Aye, *Yow*!
And on that farm he had two dogs,
and a sheep and a horse and a cow.

And a hen and a goose and a goat,
and a son called Dan,
with a wife called Nan,
and their little girl, Lucy-Anne.

And he also had a remarkable pig
called Poppy.

Everyone on the farm liked Poppy.
She was clever and kind
and very brave.

Sheep wasn't brave.
Sheep was scared of lots of things:
the farm dogs barking at her heels,

bright lights,

bang!

loud noises.

Even Sheep's shadow made
her shiver.

Oh, dear, oh, dear,
my poor old nerves.

"Fancy being
afraid of your
own shadow,"
thought Poppy.

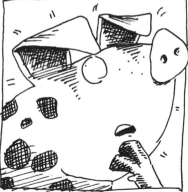

Horse was braver than Sheep.
But even Horse hid his head
in the hay when there was
thunder and lightning.

"Fancy being afraid of the weather," thought Poppy.

Cow wasn't afraid of loud noises
or bright lights.
But Cow *was* afraid of the dark.
She didn't make a fuss about it.
She just moved up closer to her
friends when darkness came.

Is there r·o·o·o·o·m for a little one?

"Fancy being afraid of the dark," thought Poppy.

Poppy wasn't afraid of
bright lights
or loud noises
or being alone in the dark.
Poppy was a plucky pig.
Everybody said so.

They said so when Poppy chased
the fox away when he tried to
gobble up Goose's goslings!

But there *was* one thing Poppy
was afraid of:
Old Man Brocksopp's pond.

Once, when Poppy was a piglet,
she'd tried to walk on water.
And she'd never forgotten it.
So Poppy kept well away from
the farm pond.

Each day, when the sun was hot,
the other animals gathered round
the pond to feel the cool breeze
coming off the water.
But Poppy didn't join them.

If Poppy had to go on errands across the farm, she took the longest route, rather than pass by the pond.

No one seemed to notice.
No one guessed Poppy's secret.
Why would they?
After all, pigs don't swim, do they?

One day, Poppy had a nasty surprise.
Old Man Brocksopp was sitting in
the yard, reading his paper.

In the paper there was a picture
of a pig, just like her.
But this pig was swimming!
"What do you think of that?"
said the farmer.
Poppy didn't know what to
think of it.
But it made her blood run cold.

That night Poppy dreamed about
the swimming pig.
She woke up in a cold sweat.
And every night that week
she had the same dream.

Poppy didn't feel at all happy.
Everyone else still thought
she was a plucky pig.
But Poppy didn't feel plucky;
she *felt* scared.

She wanted to tell someone,
but she couldn't.
Then she thought of Goat.

Goat was old and wise.
Goat would help.
Poppy decided to talk to her.
Goat didn't seem at all surprised.
"Oh, my dear," she said.
"Everyone's scared of something."
"Are they?" said Poppy.

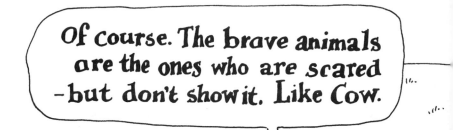

Of course. The brave animals
are the ones who are scared
-but don't show it. Like Cow.

"Cow?" said Poppy.

"Yes," said Goat. "Cow hates the dark and she has to face it every night. That's what I call brave: knowing what you're afraid of, but *not* letting it get the better of you."

Poppy went away and thought
about Goat's words.
She knew what she had to do.
The next day Poppy went to join
her friends by the pond.
Each day she moved closer
and closer to the water,
until she didn't feel so afraid.

Monday

Tuesday

Wednesday

Thursday

Friday

It was quite a hard thing to do,
but Poppy didn't tell anyone.
It was her secret.

Slowly she began to feel brave again.
She began to feel like a plucky pig.
Then, one day, something terrible
happened.

Poppy and all her friends were
snoozing in the midday sun.
Even the ducks were dreaming.
No one noticed little Lucy-Anne
trying to toddle on water.

But suddenly they heard her.
Suddenly everyone was wide awake.
Suddenly everyone went wild.

All the animals started up,
bleating and clucking
and mooing and neighing.
They didn't know what else to do,
so they all *panicked*.

But Poppy didn't panic.
She knew that someone
had to save the little girl.
Poppy, the plucky little pig,
who was *still afraid of water*,
jumped right in and
started to swim.

Boing!

Poppy didn't know how she did it.
She just did it.
She kicked her little legs
and swam to the rescue.

The other animals had made
so much noise that everyone
had come running.
Nan was there,

and Dan was there.

Even old Man Brocksopp
had heard them in the far field.
Everyone was there to see Poppy,
the pluckiest pig in the world,
save little Lucy-Anne from drowning.

None of them realised why this
was Poppy's bravest deed of all,
except Goat, of course.
And Goat knew how to keep a secret.

Other great ANIMAL CRACKERS